TAO
The Little Samurai

#4

The Championship!

Laurent Richard
illustrated by **Nicolas Ryser**
Translation: **Edward Gauvin**

GRAPHIC UNIVERSE™ • MINNEAPOLIS

STORY BY LAURENT RICHARD
ILLUSTRATIONS BY NICOLAS RYSER
COLORING BY STEVAN ROUDAUT
TRANSLATION BY EDWARD GAUVIN

FIRST AMERICAN EDITION PUBLISHED IN 2014 BY GRAPHIC UNIVERSE™.

AU CHAMPIONNAT D'ARTS MARTIAUX BY LAURENT RICHARD AND NICOLAS RYSER © BAYARD ÉDITIONS, 2011
COPYRIGHT © 2014 BY LERNER PUBLISHING GROUP, INC., FOR THE US EDITION

GRAPHIC UNIVERSE™ IS A TRADEMARK OF LERNER PUBLISHING GROUP, INC.

GRAPHIC UNIVERSE™
A DIVISION OF LERNER PUBLISHING GROUP, INC.
241 FIRST AVENUE NORTH
MINNEAPOLIS, MN 55401 USA

FOR READING LEVELS AND MORE INFORMATION,
LOOK UP THIS TITLE AT WWW.LERNERBOOKS.COM.

MAIN BODY TEXT SET IN CCWILDWORDS 8.5/10.5.
TYPEFACE PROVIDED BY FONTOGRAPHER.

LIBRARY OF CONGRESS CATALOGING-IN-PUBLICATION DATA

RICHARD, LAURENT, 1968–
    [AU CHAMPIONNAT D'ARTS MARTIAUX. ENGLISH]
    THE CHAMPIONSHIP! / BY LAURENT RICHARD ; ILLUSTRATED BY NICOLAS RYSER ; TRANSLATION:
EDWARD GAUVIN. – FIRST AMERICAN EDITION.
        P.   CM. – (TAO, THE LITTLE SAMURAI ; #4)
    SUMMARY: THE STUDENTS OF MASTER SNOW'S DOJO ARE EXCITED ABOUT THEIR TRIP TO THE
INTERNATIONAL MARTIAL ARTS CHAMPIONSHIP, BUT UPON ARRIVAL TWO OF THE BEST FIGHTERS IN
THE SCHOOL'S HISTORY, HIRO AND JAY, DISAPPEAR.
    ISBN 978-1-4677-2097-7 (LIB. BDG. : ALK. PAPER)
    ISBN 978-1-4677-4661-8 (EBOOK)
    1. GRAPHIC NOVELS. [1. GRAPHIC NOVELS. 2. MARTIAL ARTS–FICTION. 3. SAMURAI–FICTION.
4. KIDNAPPING–FICTION. 5. ROBBERS AND OUTLAWS–FICTION.] I. RYSER, NICOLAS, ILLUSTRATOR.
II. GAUVIN, EDWARD, TRANSLATOR. III. TITLE.
PZ7.7.RSCH 2014
741.5'944–DC23   2013038066

MANUFACTURED IN THE UNITED STATES OF AMERICA
1 - VI - 7/15/14

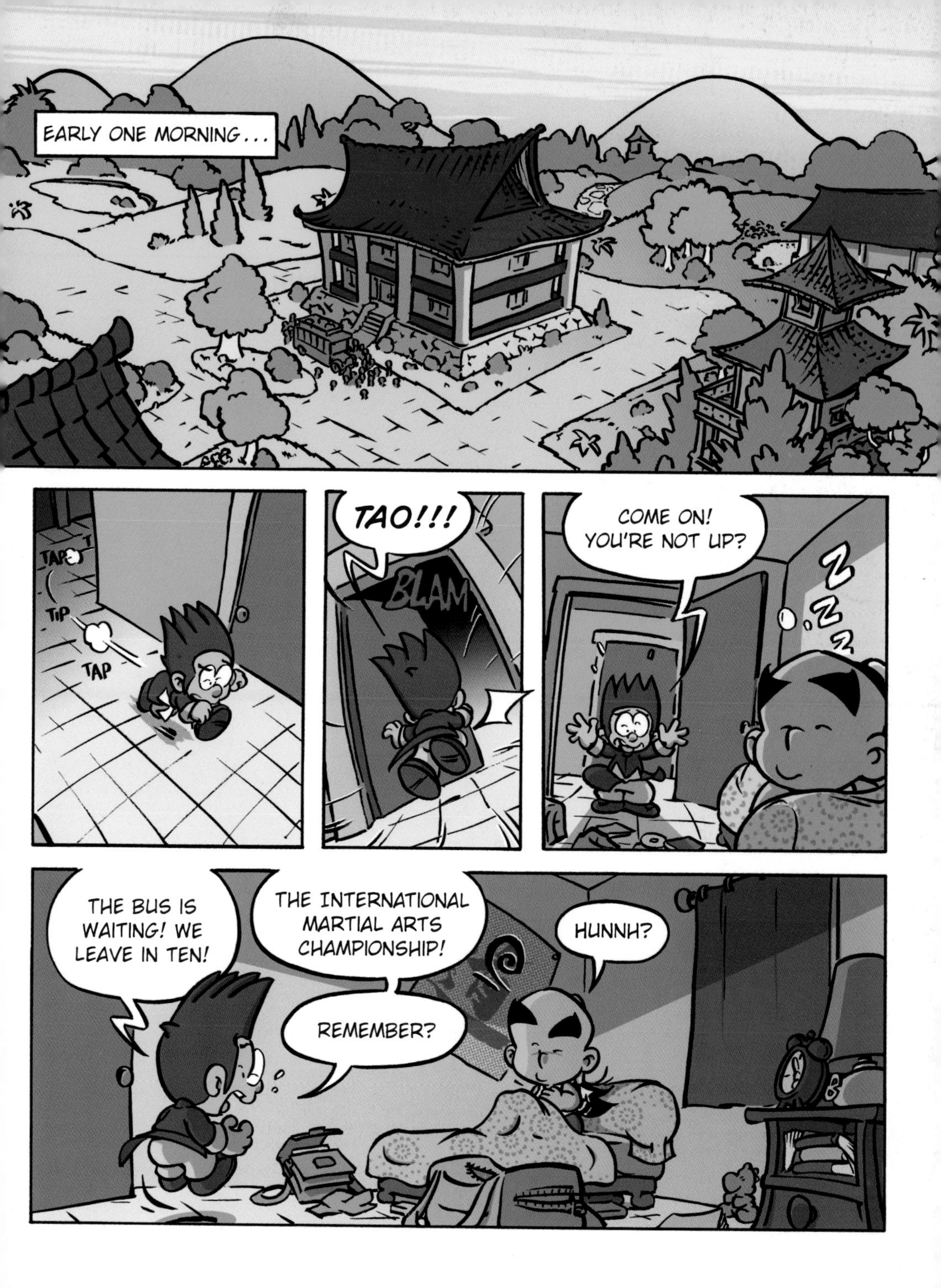
EARLY ONE MORNING...
TAP
TIP
TAP
TAO!!!
BLAM
COME ON! YOU'RE NOT UP?
Z Z Z
THE BUS IS WAITING! WE LEAVE IN TEN!
THE INTERNATIONAL MARTIAL ARTS CHAMPIONSHIP!
REMEMBER?
HUNNH?

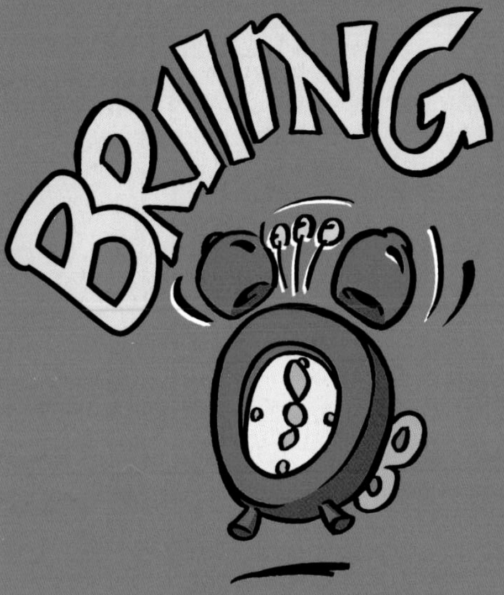
BRIING

Let's
Go!

MY ENEMY, MASTER SNOW, HAS NO IDEA WHAT AWAITS HIM.

SNOW'S KIDS WON'T WIN A SINGLE MEDAL! PROCEED WITH YOUR MISSION!

HEH HEH. GREAT IDEA, MASTER! TRULY DIABOLICAL!

WE'LL GET 'EM NOW!

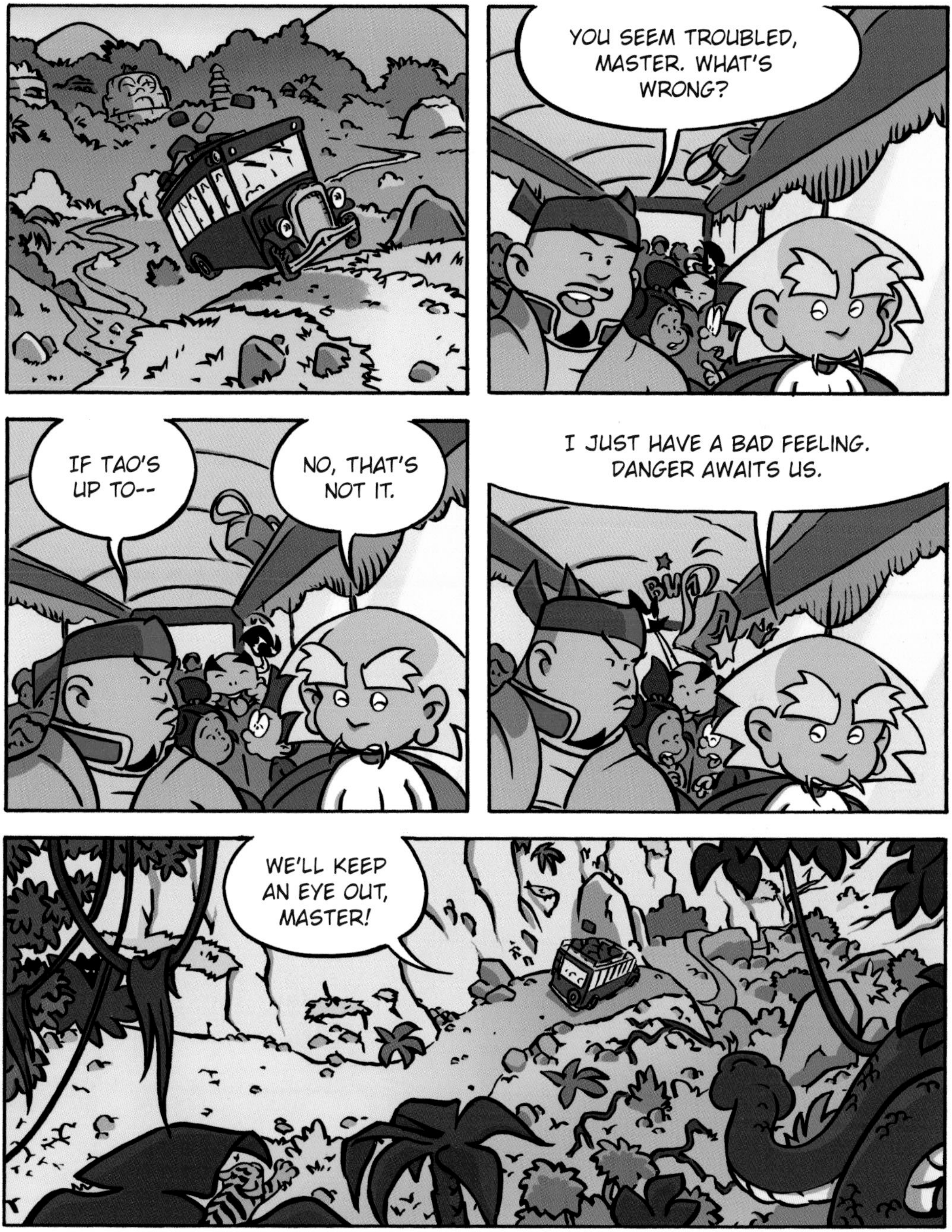
YOU SEEM TROUBLED, MASTER. WHAT'S WRONG?
IF TAO'S UP TO--
NO, THAT'S NOT IT.
I JUST HAVE A BAD FEELING. DANGER AWAITS US.
WE'LL KEEP AN EYE OUT, MASTER!

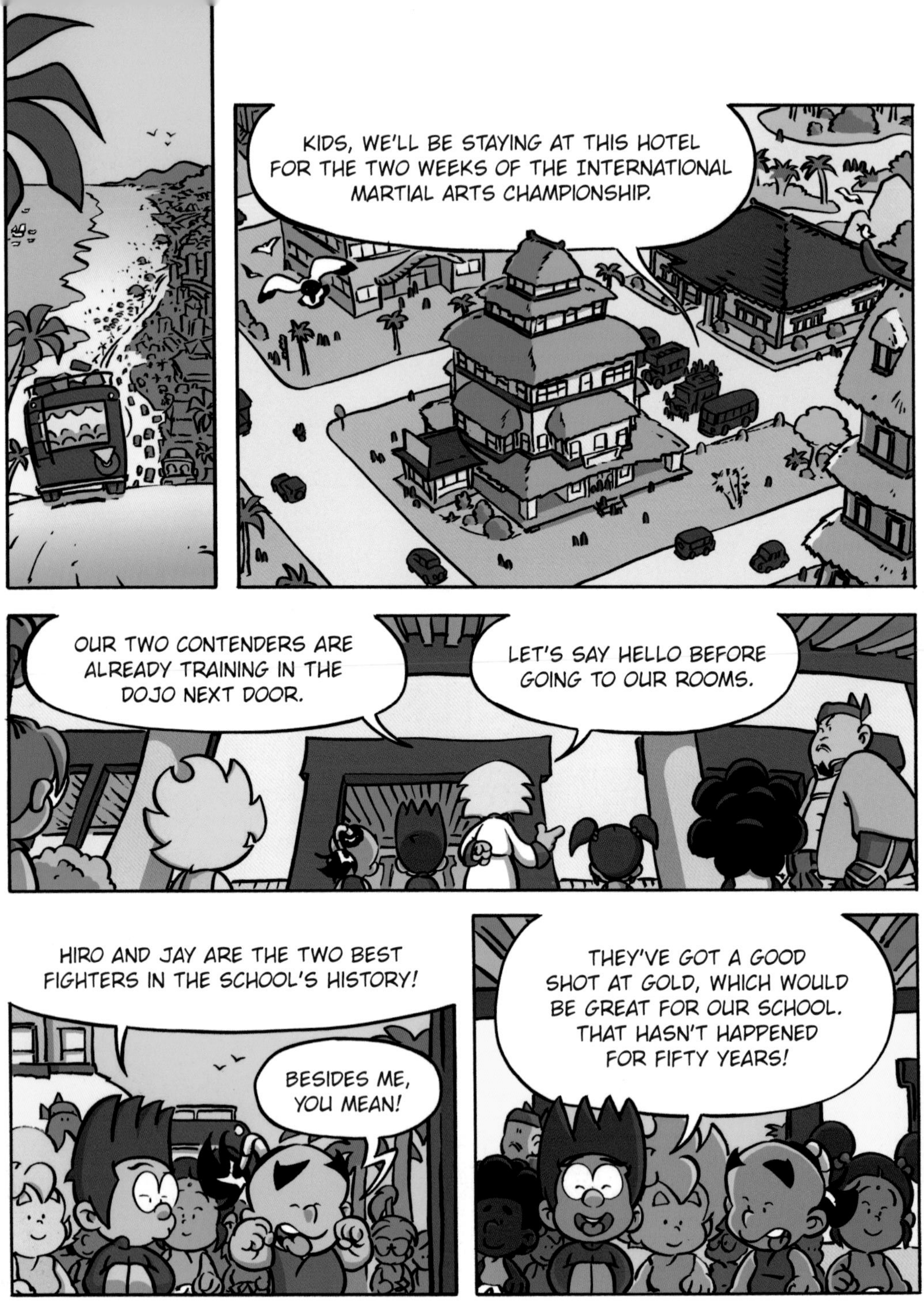
KIDS, WE'LL BE STAYING AT THIS HOTEL FOR THE TWO WEEKS OF THE INTERNATIONAL MARTIAL ARTS CHAMPIONSHIP.
OUR TWO CONTENDERS ARE ALREADY TRAINING IN THE DOJO NEXT DOOR.
LET'S SAY HELLO BEFORE GOING TO OUR ROOMS.
HIRO AND JAY ARE THE TWO BEST FIGHTERS IN THE SCHOOL'S HISTORY!
BESIDES ME, YOU MEAN!
THEY'VE GOT A GOOD SHOT AT GOLD, WHICH WOULD BE GREAT FOR OUR SCHOOL. THAT HASN'T HAPPENED FOR FIFTY YEARS!

11

The mystery!

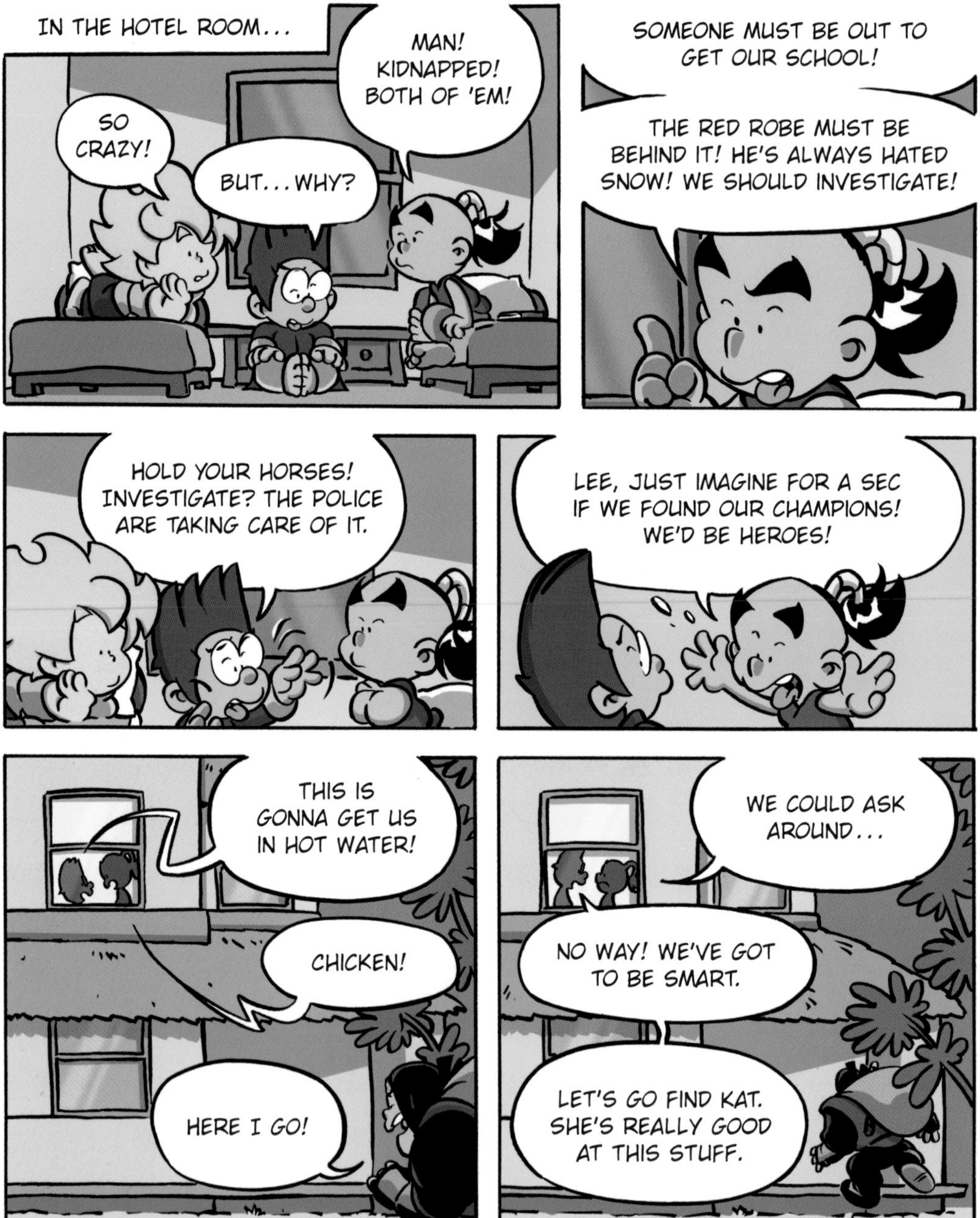
IN THE HOTEL ROOM...
MAN! KIDNAPPED! BOTH OF 'EM!
SO CRAZY!
BUT...WHY?
SOMEONE MUST BE OUT TO GET OUR SCHOOL!
THE RED ROBE MUST BE BEHIND IT! HE'S ALWAYS HATED SNOW! WE SHOULD INVESTIGATE!
HOLD YOUR HORSES! INVESTIGATE? THE POLICE ARE TAKING CARE OF IT.
LEE, JUST IMAGINE FOR A SEC IF WE FOUND OUR CHAMPIONS! WE'D BE HEROES!
THIS IS GONNA GET US IN HOT WATER!
CHICKEN!
HERE I GO!
WE COULD ASK AROUND...
NO WAY! WE'VE GOT TO BE SMART.
LET'S GO FIND KAT. SHE'S REALLY GOOD AT THIS STUFF.

FIRST, WE'LL EXAMINE THEIR ROOM.

ULP! THE POLICE BLOCKED IT OFF!

POLICE LINE D

C'MON, NO ONE'S THERE. LET'S TAKE A QUICK LOOK!

WELL?

I MIGHT'VE FOUND SOMETHING.

HURRY! SOMEONE'S COMING!

MEET UP TOMORROW BEFORE BREAKFAST!

15

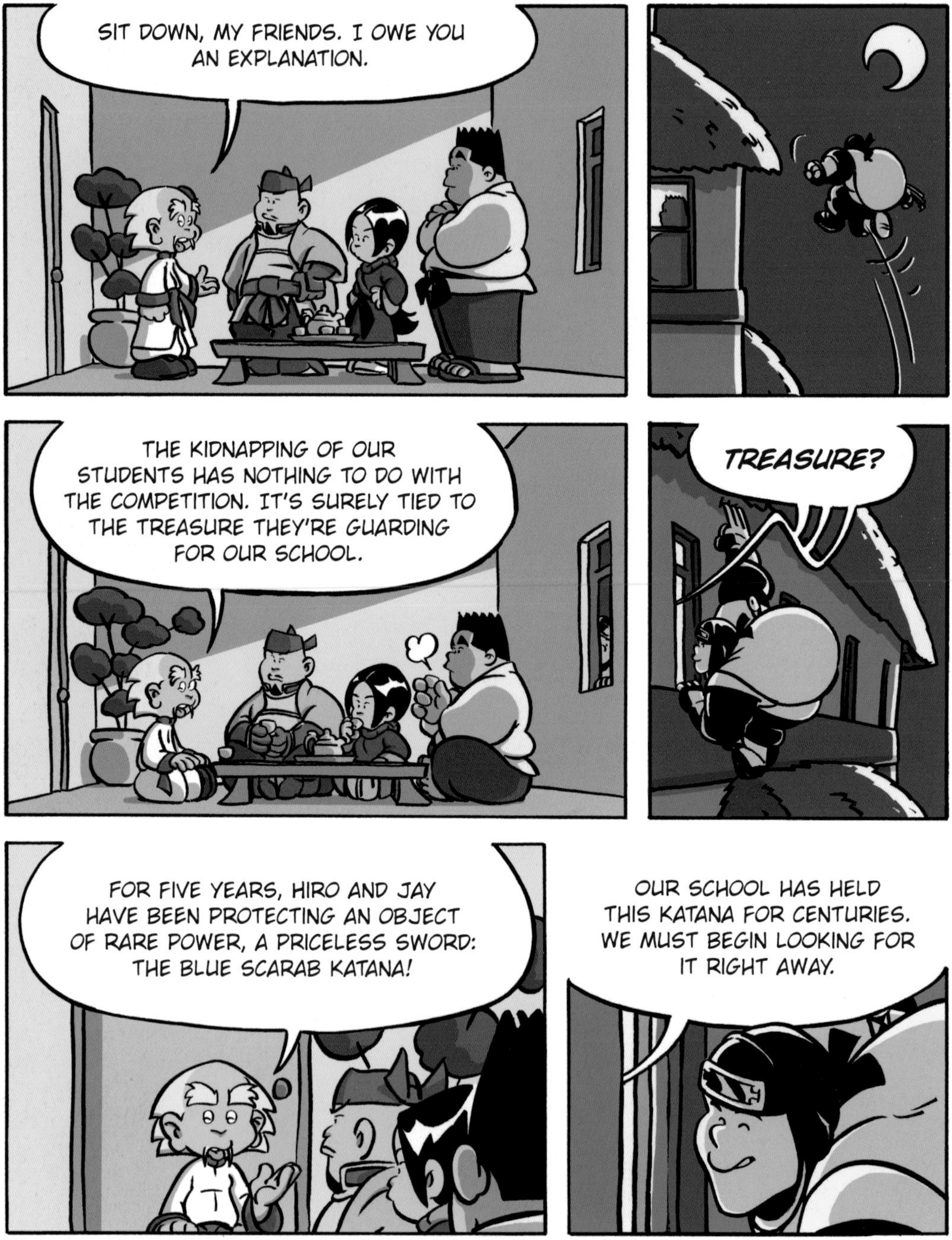
SIT DOWN, MY FRIENDS. I OWE YOU AN EXPLANATION.
THE KIDNAPPING OF OUR STUDENTS HAS NOTHING TO DO WITH THE COMPETITION. IT'S SURELY TIED TO THE TREASURE THEY'RE GUARDING FOR OUR SCHOOL.
TREASURE?
FOR FIVE YEARS, HIRO AND JAY HAVE BEEN PROTECTING AN OBJECT OF RARE POWER, A PRICELESS SWORD: THE BLUE SCARAB KATANA!
OUR SCHOOL HAS HELD THIS KATANA FOR CENTURIES. WE MUST BEGIN LOOKING FOR IT RIGHT AWAY.

OUR SITUATION IS VERY SERIOUS. I FEAR FOR OUR STUDENTS' LIVES AND THE SCHOOL'S FUTURE. GO, QUICKLY! I'LL SEE TO THE CHILDREN.

GOOD LUCK.

HEH! JUST TOO EASY!

MORNING . . .

SO, WHAT DO WE DO NOW?

CHECK OUT MY PHOTOS FROM LAST NIGHT.

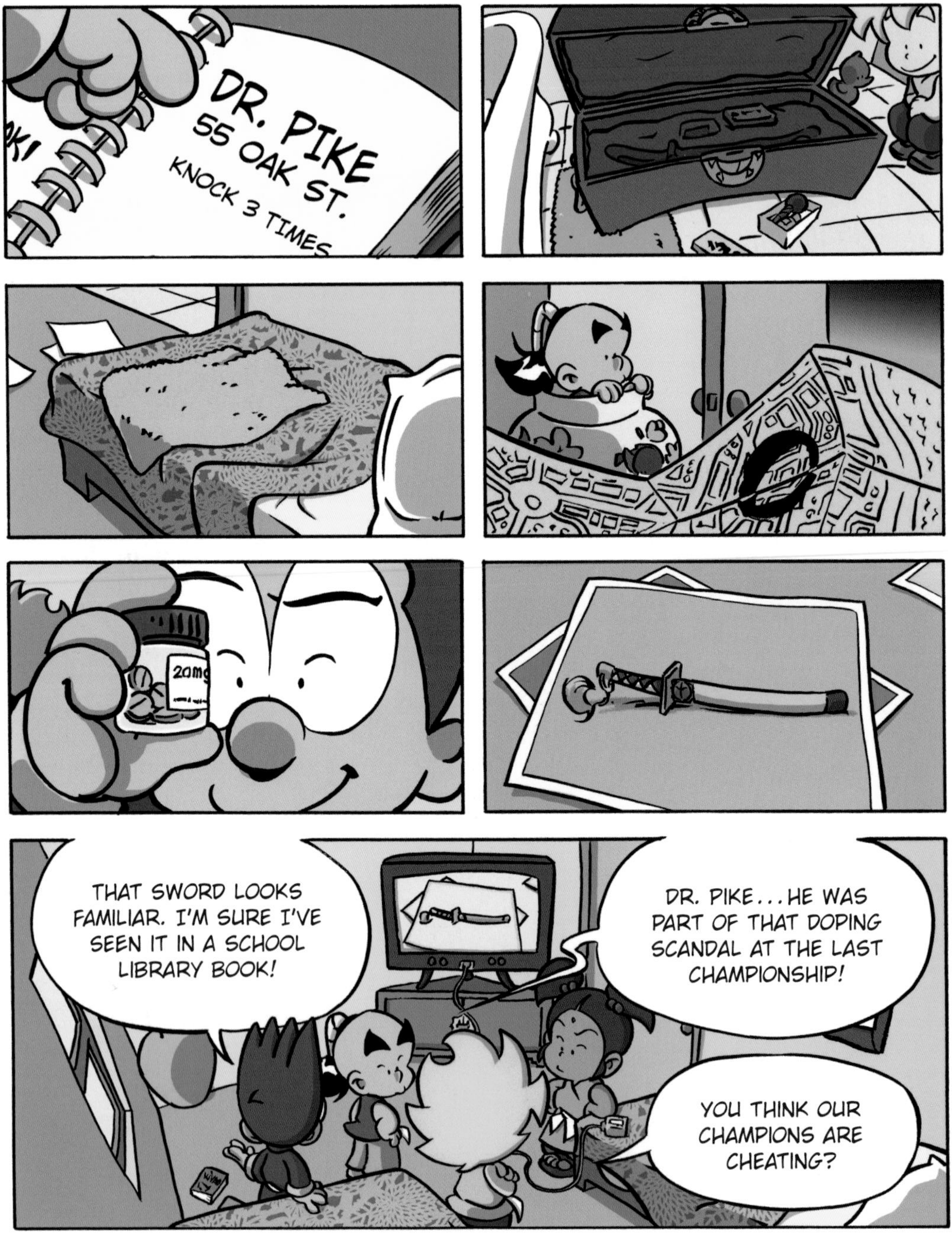
DR. PIKE
55 OAK ST.
KNOCK 3 TIMES
20mg
THAT SWORD LOOKS FAMILIAR. I'M SURE I'VE SEEN IT IN A SCHOOL LIBRARY BOOK!
DR. PIKE... HE WAS PART OF THAT DOPING SCANDAL AT THE LAST CHAMPIONSHIP!
YOU THINK OUR CHAMPIONS ARE CHEATING?

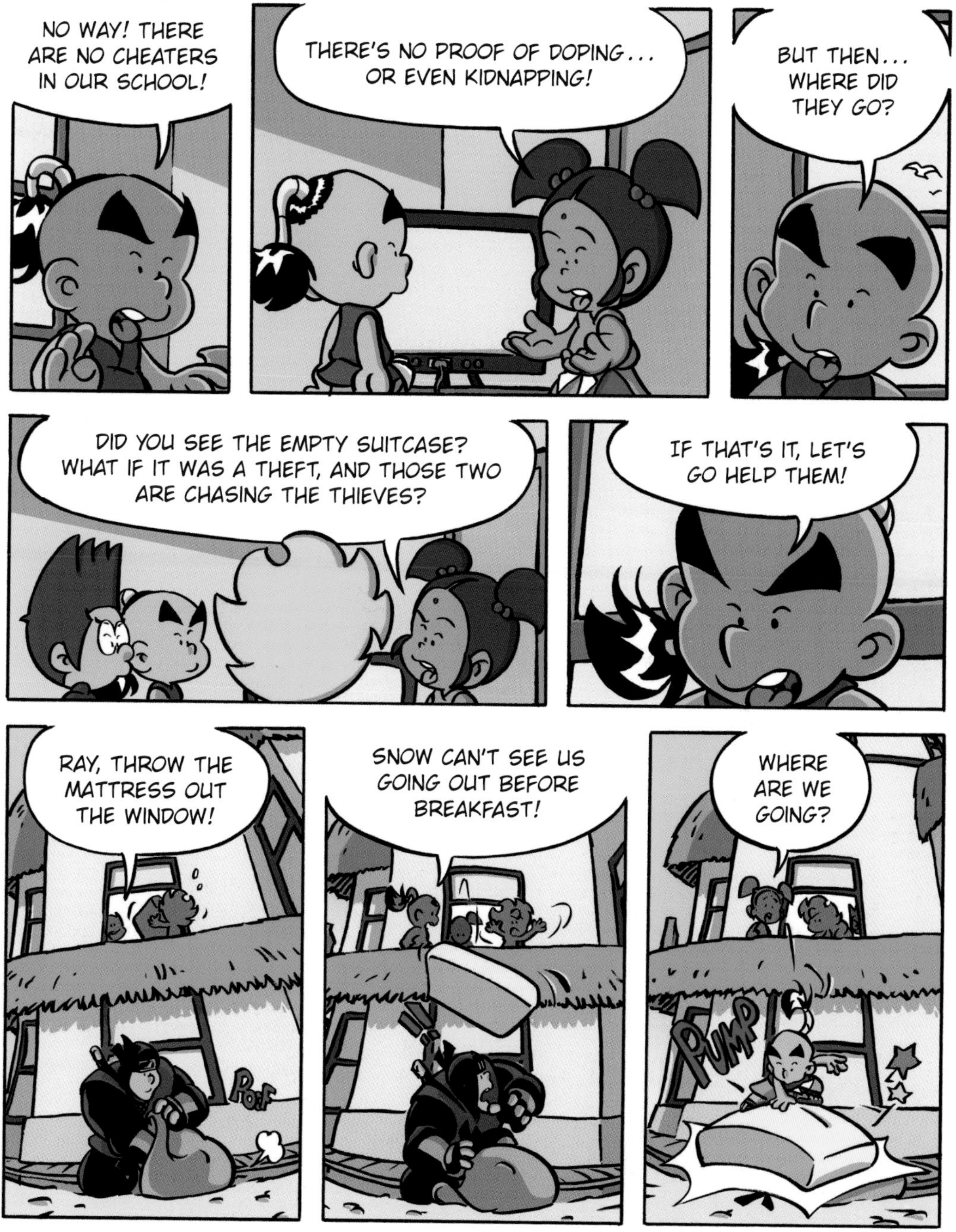
NO WAY! THERE ARE NO CHEATERS IN OUR SCHOOL!
THERE'S NO PROOF OF DOPING... OR EVEN KIDNAPPING!
BUT THEN... WHERE DID THEY GO?
DID YOU SEE THE EMPTY SUITCASE? WHAT IF IT WAS A THEFT, AND THOSE TWO ARE CHASING THE THIEVES?
IF THAT'S IT, LET'S GO HELP THEM!
RAY, THROW THE MATTRESS OUT THE WINDOW!
POOF
SNOW CAN'T SEE US GOING OUT BEFORE BREAKFAST!
WHERE ARE WE GOING?
PUMP

The Investigation!

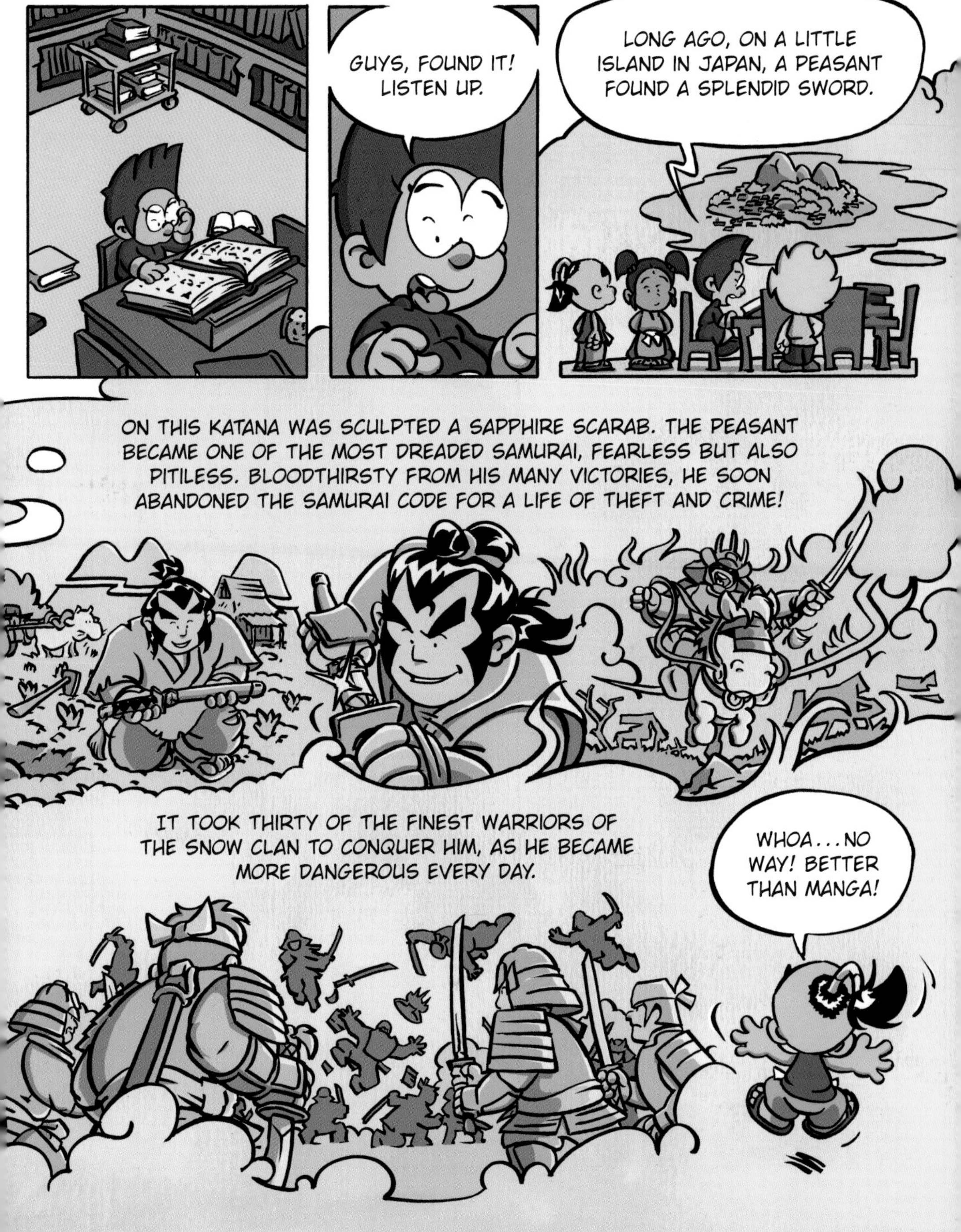

GUYS, FOUND IT! LISTEN UP.
LONG AGO, ON A LITTLE ISLAND IN JAPAN, A PEASANT FOUND A SPLENDID SWORD.
ON THIS KATANA WAS SCULPTED A SAPPHIRE SCARAB. THE PEASANT BECAME ONE OF THE MOST DREADED SAMURAI, FEARLESS BUT ALSO PITILESS. BLOODTHIRSTY FROM HIS MANY VICTORIES, HE SOON ABANDONED THE SAMURAI CODE FOR A LIFE OF THEFT AND CRIME!
IT TOOK THIRTY OF THE FINEST WARRIORS OF THE SNOW CLAN TO CONQUER HIM, AS HE BECAME MORE DANGEROUS EVERY DAY.
WHOA . . . NO WAY! BETTER THAN MANGA!

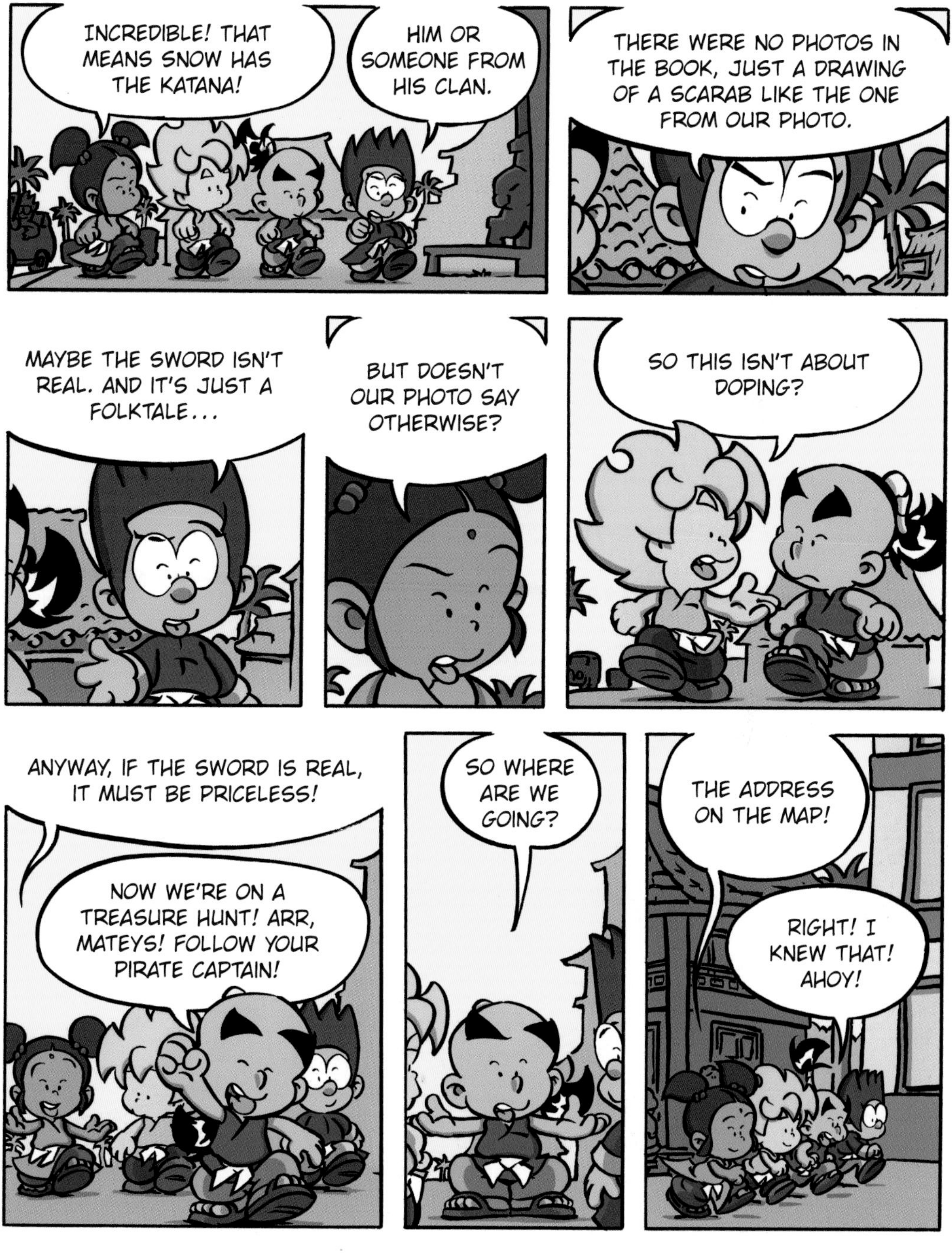
INCREDIBLE! THAT MEANS SNOW HAS THE KATANA!
HIM OR SOMEONE FROM HIS CLAN.
THERE WERE NO PHOTOS IN THE BOOK, JUST A DRAWING OF A SCARAB LIKE THE ONE FROM OUR PHOTO.
MAYBE THE SWORD ISN'T REAL. AND IT'S JUST A FOLKTALE...
BUT DOESN'T OUR PHOTO SAY OTHERWISE?
SO THIS ISN'T ABOUT DOPING?
ANYWAY, IF THE SWORD IS REAL, IT MUST BE PRICELESS!
NOW WE'RE ON A TREASURE HUNT! ARR, MATEYS! FOLLOW YOUR PIRATE CAPTAIN!
SO WHERE ARE WE GOING?
THE ADDRESS ON THE MAP!
RIGHT! I KNEW THAT! AHOY!

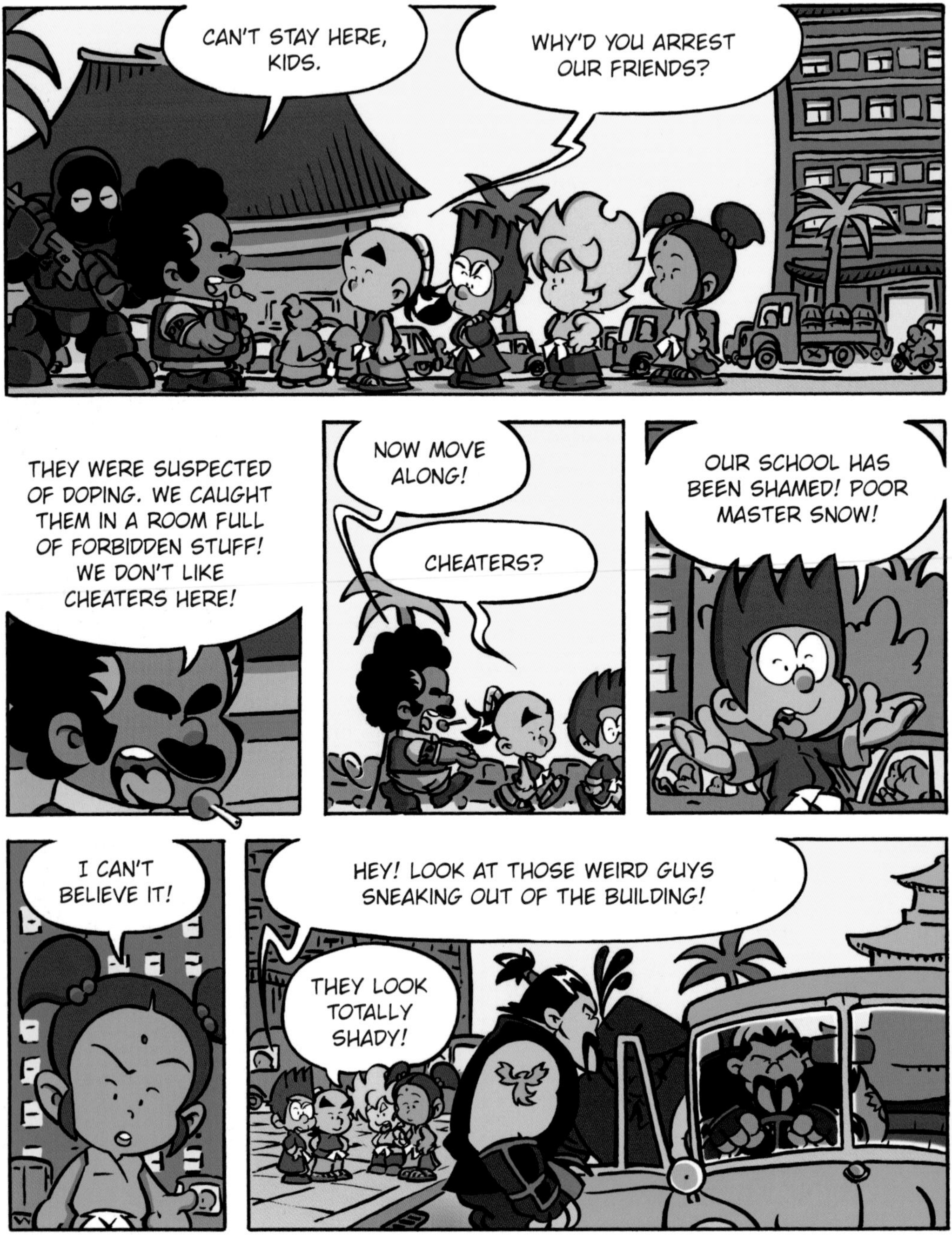
CAN'T STAY HERE, KIDS.
WHY'D YOU ARREST OUR FRIENDS?
THEY WERE SUSPECTED OF DOPING. WE CAUGHT THEM IN A ROOM FULL OF FORBIDDEN STUFF! WE DON'T LIKE CHEATERS HERE!
NOW MOVE ALONG!
CHEATERS?
OUR SCHOOL HAS BEEN SHAMED! POOR MASTER SNOW!
I CAN'T BELIEVE IT!
HEY! LOOK AT THOSE WEIRD GUYS SNEAKING OUT OF THE BUILDING!
THEY LOOK TOTALLY SHADY!

29

30

The phoenix Clan

A FEW MINUTES LATER, OUR FRIENDS HAD SHARED THEIR INCREDIBLE MORNING!

FORGET IT! WE'VE MADE A FOOL OF SNOW! HIS CHAMPIONS ARE IN PRISON!

IT WASN'T OUR PLAN THAT PUT THEM THERE, BUT WHO CARES?

AS FOR OUR PLAN...WHAT DID YOU DO WITH ALL OUR LITTLE GAS CAPSULES?

OH, THE CAPSULES! I KEPT THEM, SINCE THERE WAS NO ONE AROUND.

PSSSHHHH

FOOL! THEY'LL--

PSSSHHHH

CHILDREN, YOU'VE BEEN VERY BRAVE!

POF POF POF POF POF POF

35

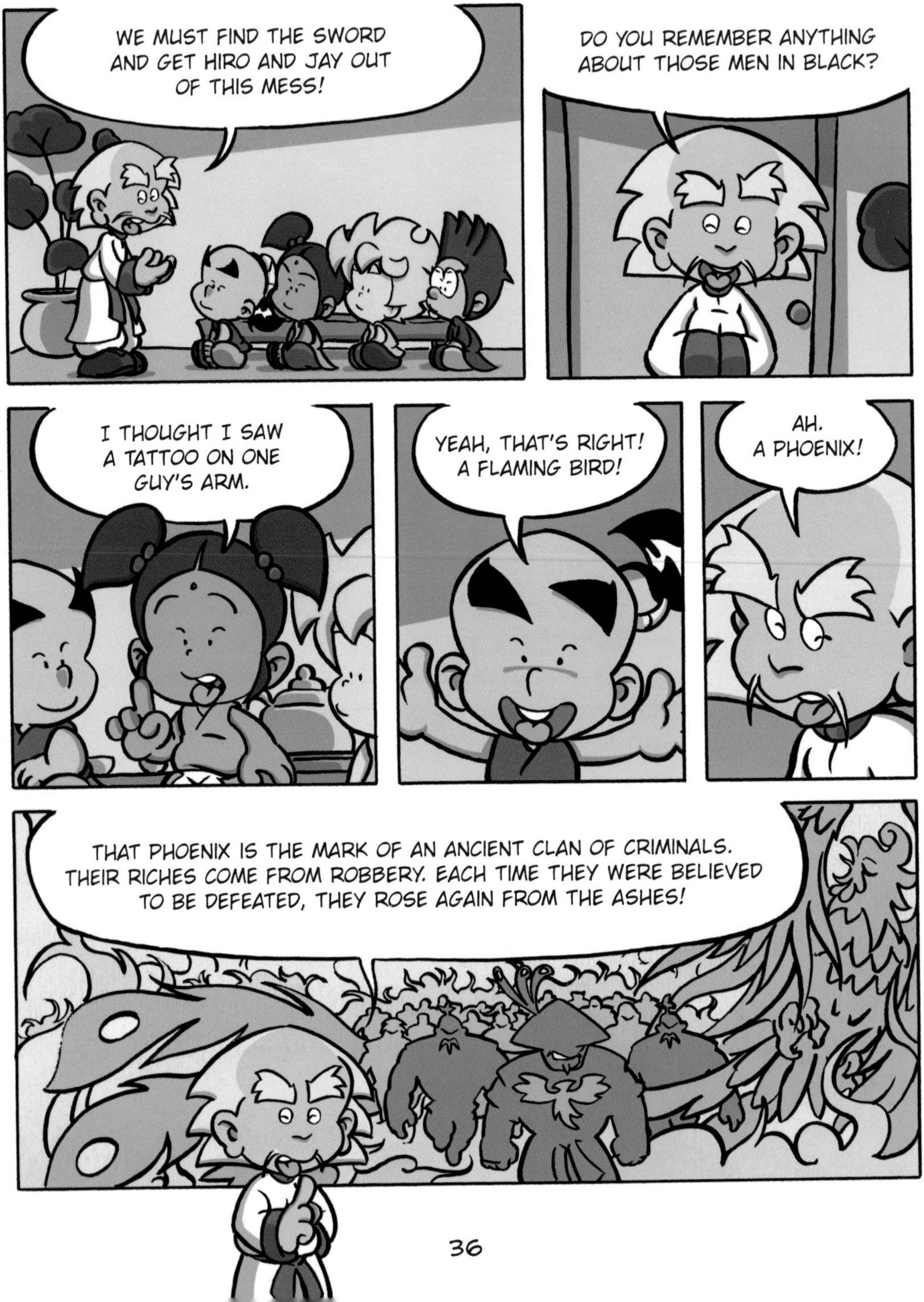

WE MUST FIND THE SWORD AND GET HIRO AND JAY OUT OF THIS MESS!
DO YOU REMEMBER ANYTHING ABOUT THOSE MEN IN BLACK?
I THOUGHT I SAW A TATTOO ON ONE GUY'S ARM.
YEAH, THAT'S RIGHT! A FLAMING BIRD!
AH. A PHOENIX!
THAT PHOENIX IS THE MARK OF AN ANCIENT CLAN OF CRIMINALS. THEIR RICHES COME FROM ROBBERY. EACH TIME THEY WERE BELIEVED TO BE DEFEATED, THEY ROSE AGAIN FROM THE ASHES!

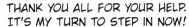

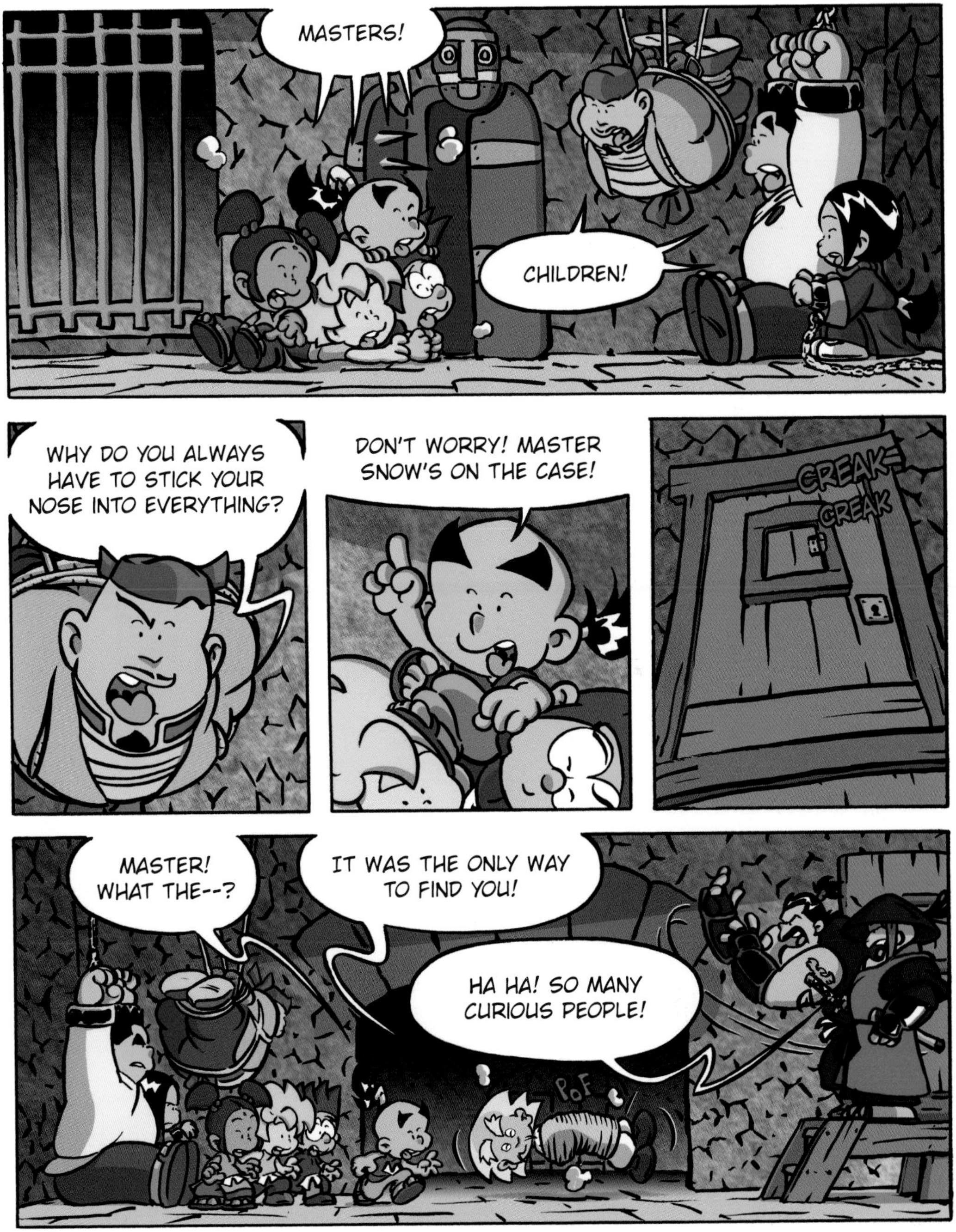

MASTERS!
CHILDREN!
WHY DO YOU ALWAYS HAVE TO STICK YOUR NOSE INTO EVERYTHING?
DON'T WORRY! MASTER SNOW'S ON THE CASE!
CREAK
CREAK
MASTER! WHAT THE--?
IT WAS THE ONLY WAY TO FIND YOU!
HA HA! SO MANY CURIOUS PEOPLE!
POF

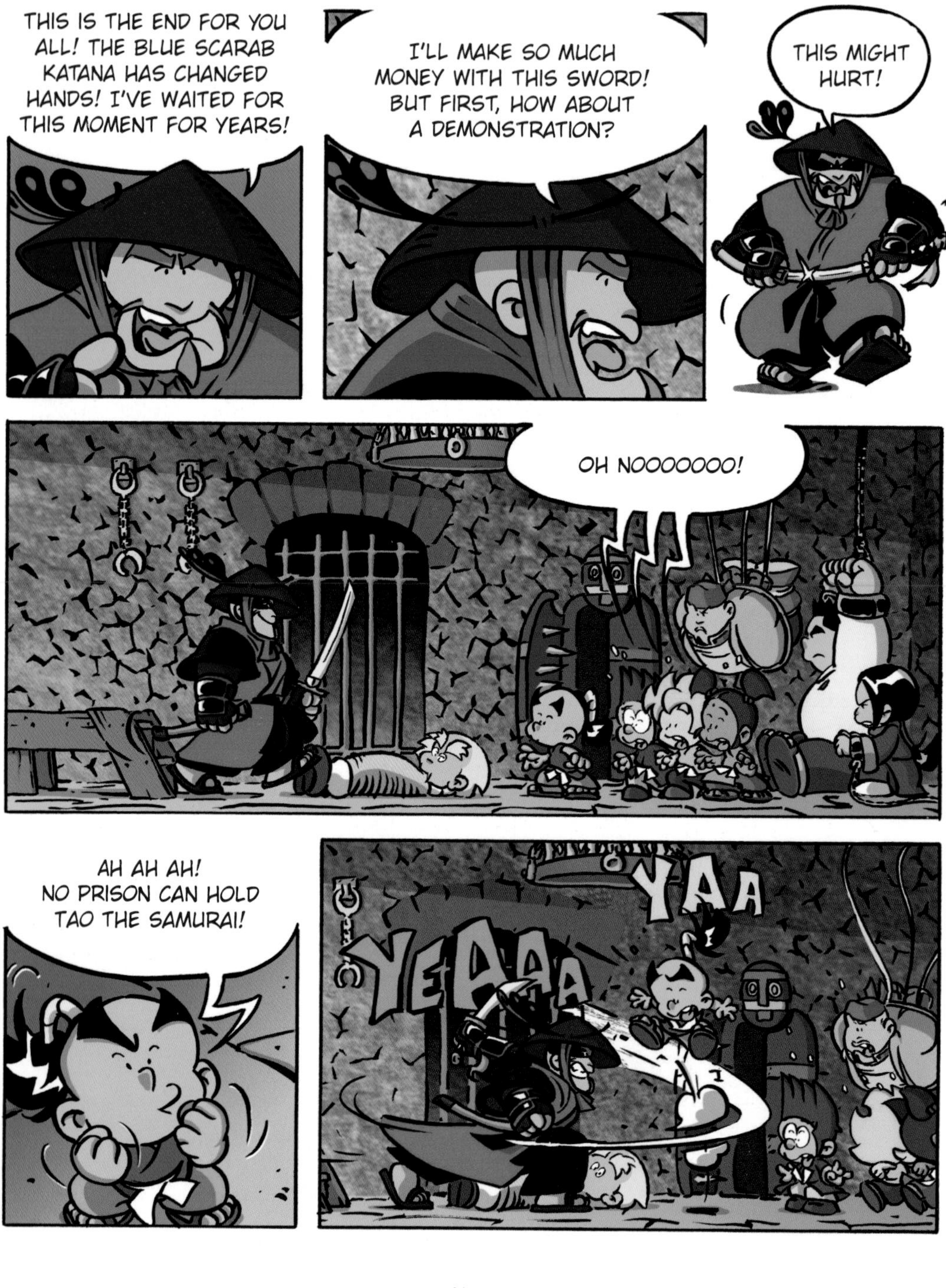
THIS IS THE END FOR YOU ALL! THE BLUE SCARAB KATANA HAS CHANGED HANDS! I'VE WAITED FOR THIS MOMENT FOR YEARS!
I'LL MAKE SO MUCH MONEY WITH THIS SWORD! BUT FIRST, HOW ABOUT A DEMONSTRATION?
THIS MIGHT HURT!
OH NOOOOOOO!
AH AH AH! NO PRISON CAN HOLD TAO THE SAMURAI!
YEAAA
YAA

41

42

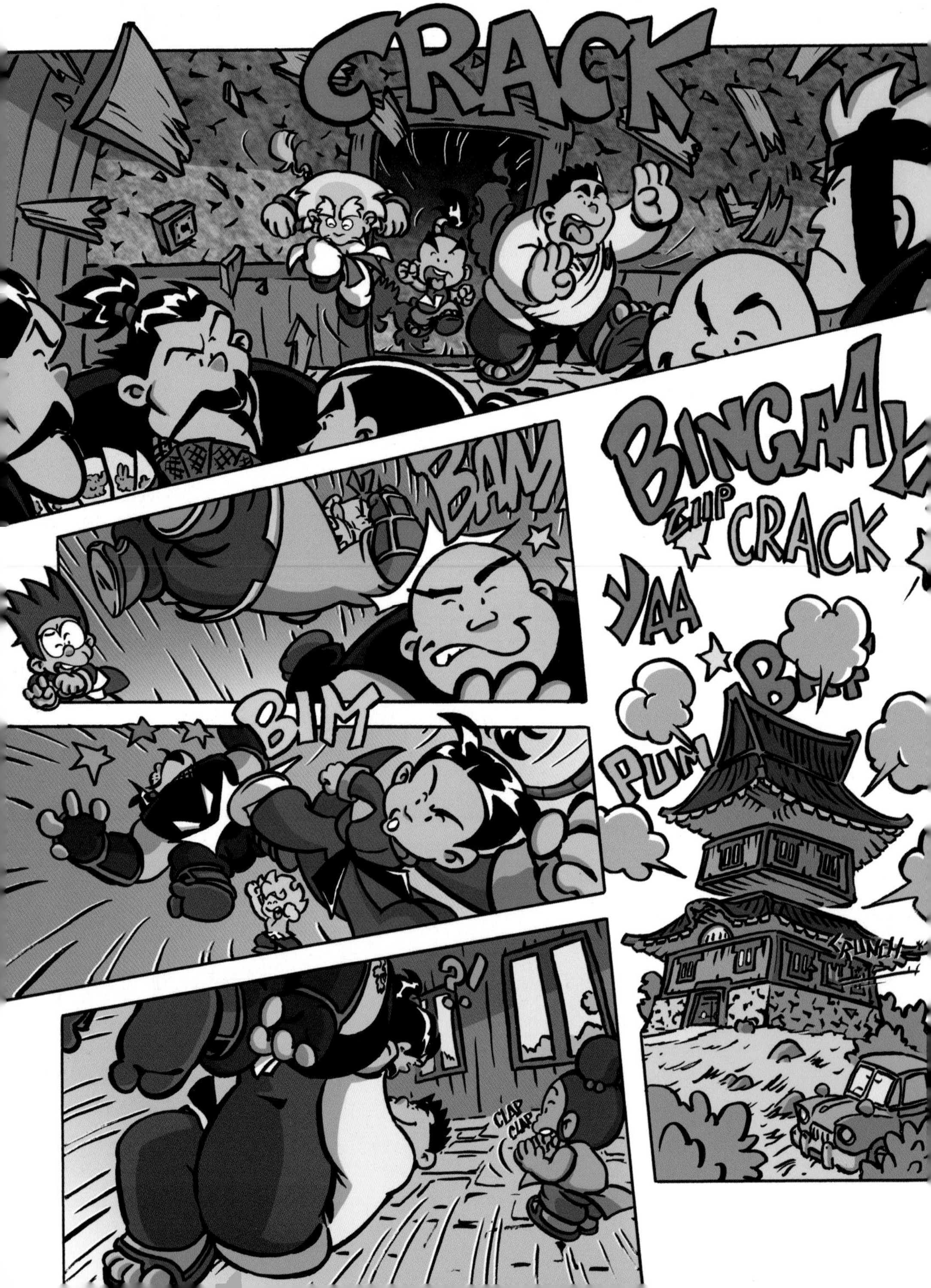

CRACK
BAM
BINGAAY
ZIP
CRACK
YAA
PUM
BIM
?!
CLAP
CLAP
CRUNCH

I THINK THEY LEARNED THEIR LESSON!

YOU CAN STOP, TAO!

The Final Chapter

HALF AN HOUR LATER...

BRAVO, MASTER! WITH YOUR HELP, WE FINALLY NABBED 'EM! YOU'VE BROUGHT DOWN A DANGEROUS CRIMINAL ORGANIZATION!

I'LL FREE YOUR CHAMPIONS RIGHT AWAY!

THANK YOU...

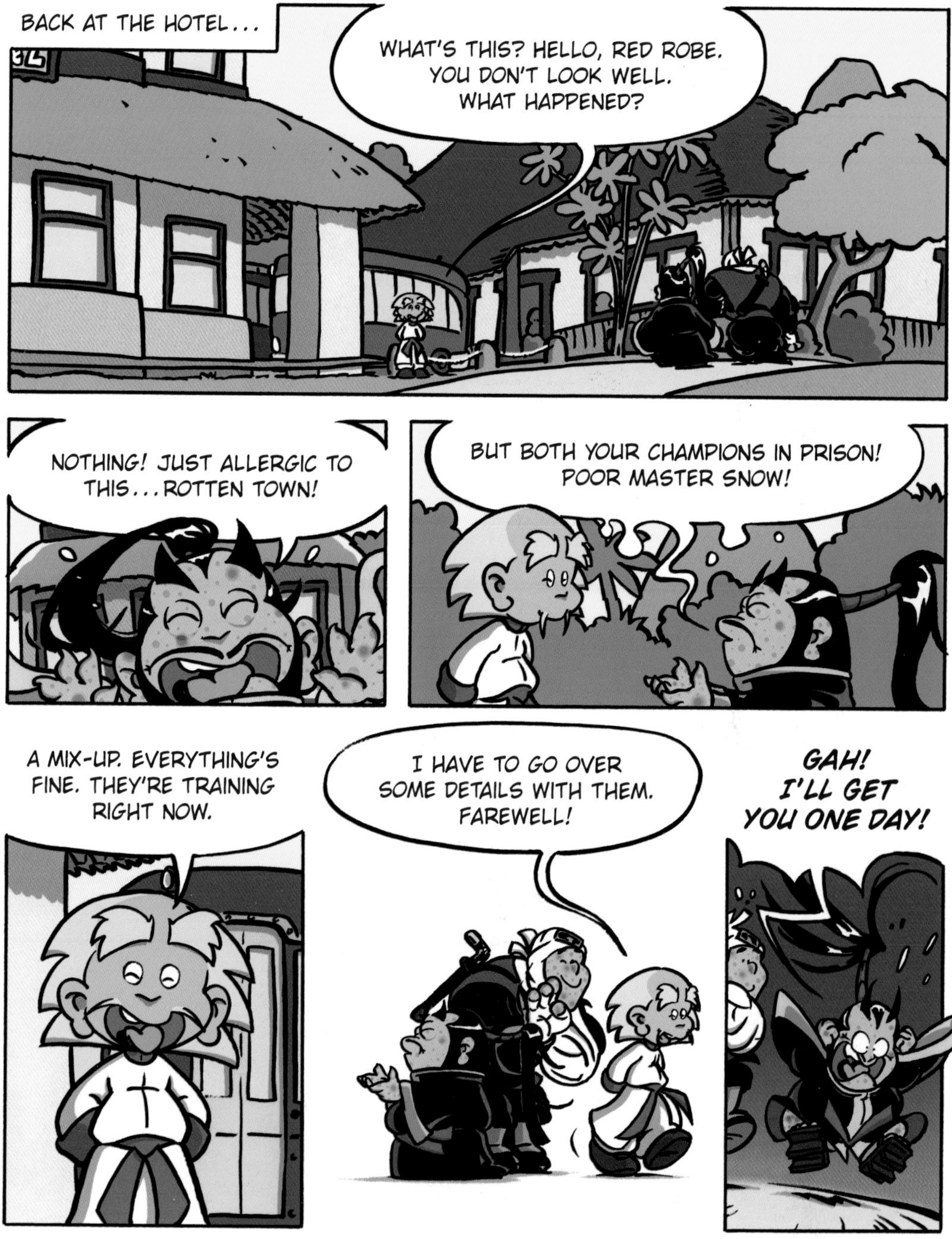
BACK AT THE HOTEL...
WHAT'S THIS? HELLO, RED ROBE. YOU DON'T LOOK WELL. WHAT HAPPENED?
NOTHING! JUST ALLERGIC TO THIS...ROTTEN TOWN!
BUT BOTH YOUR CHAMPIONS IN PRISON! POOR MASTER SNOW!
A MIX-UP. EVERYTHING'S FINE. THEY'RE TRAINING RIGHT NOW.
I HAVE TO GO OVER SOME DETAILS WITH THEM. FAREWELL!
GAH! I'LL GET YOU ONE DAY!

THE NEXT DAY...

IT'S UP TO YOU NOW, FRIENDS!

BUT KNOW THIS.

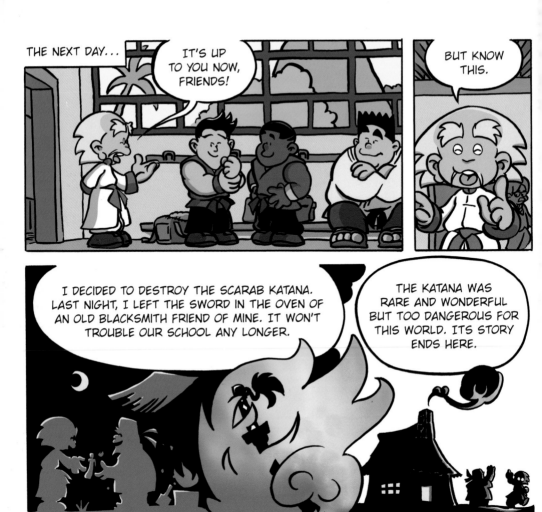

I DECIDED TO DESTROY THE SCARAB KATANA. LAST NIGHT, I LEFT THE SWORD IN THE OVEN OF AN OLD BLACKSMITH FRIEND OF MINE. IT WON'T TROUBLE OUR SCHOOL ANY LONGER.

THE KATANA WAS RARE AND WONDERFUL BUT TOO DANGEROUS FOR THIS WORLD. ITS STORY ENDS HERE.

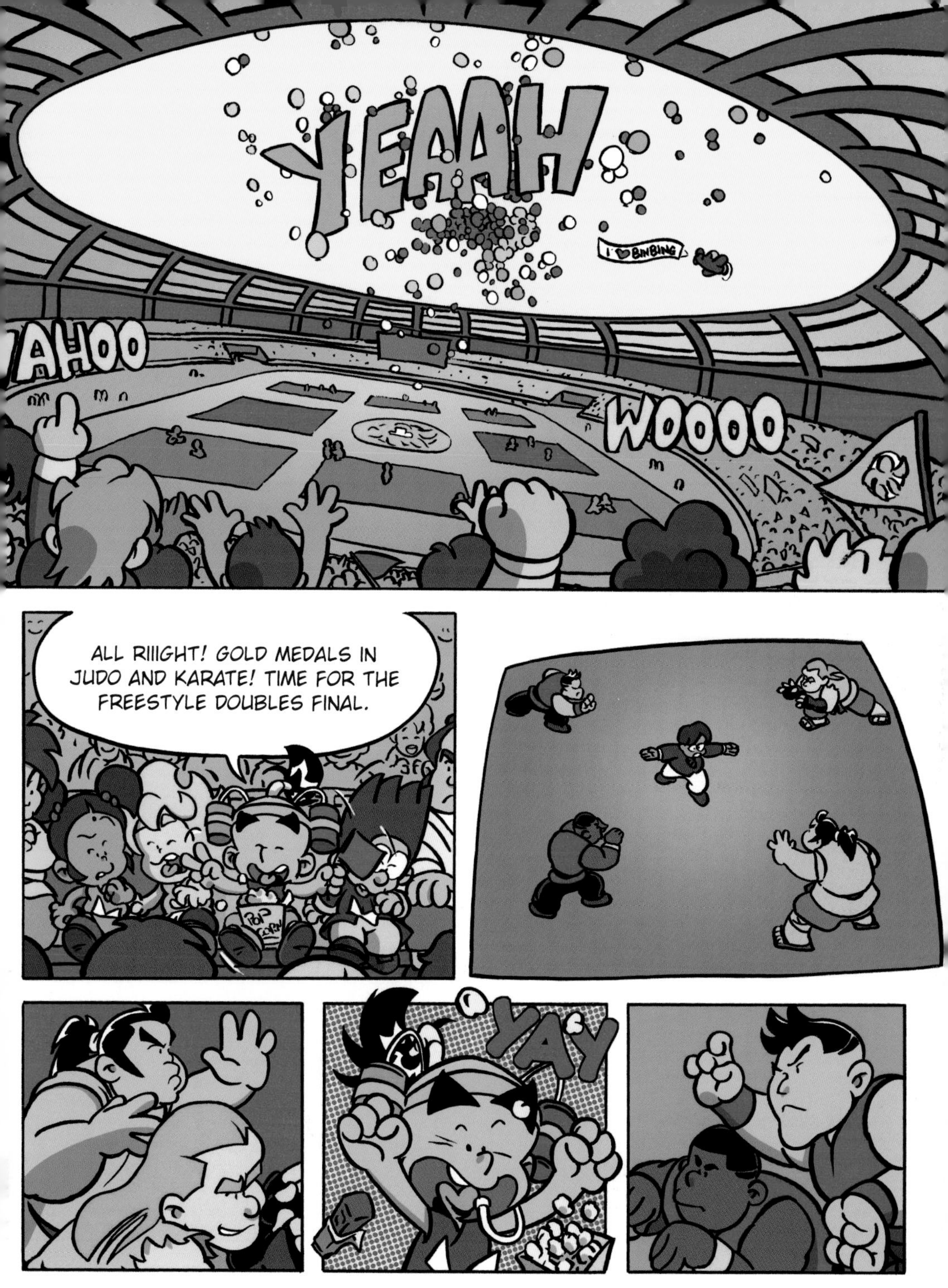
YEAAH
I ♥ BINBING
AHOO
WOOOO
ALL RIIIGHT! GOLD MEDALS IN JUDO AND KARATE! TIME FOR THE FREESTYLE DOUBLES FINAL.
POP CORN
YAY

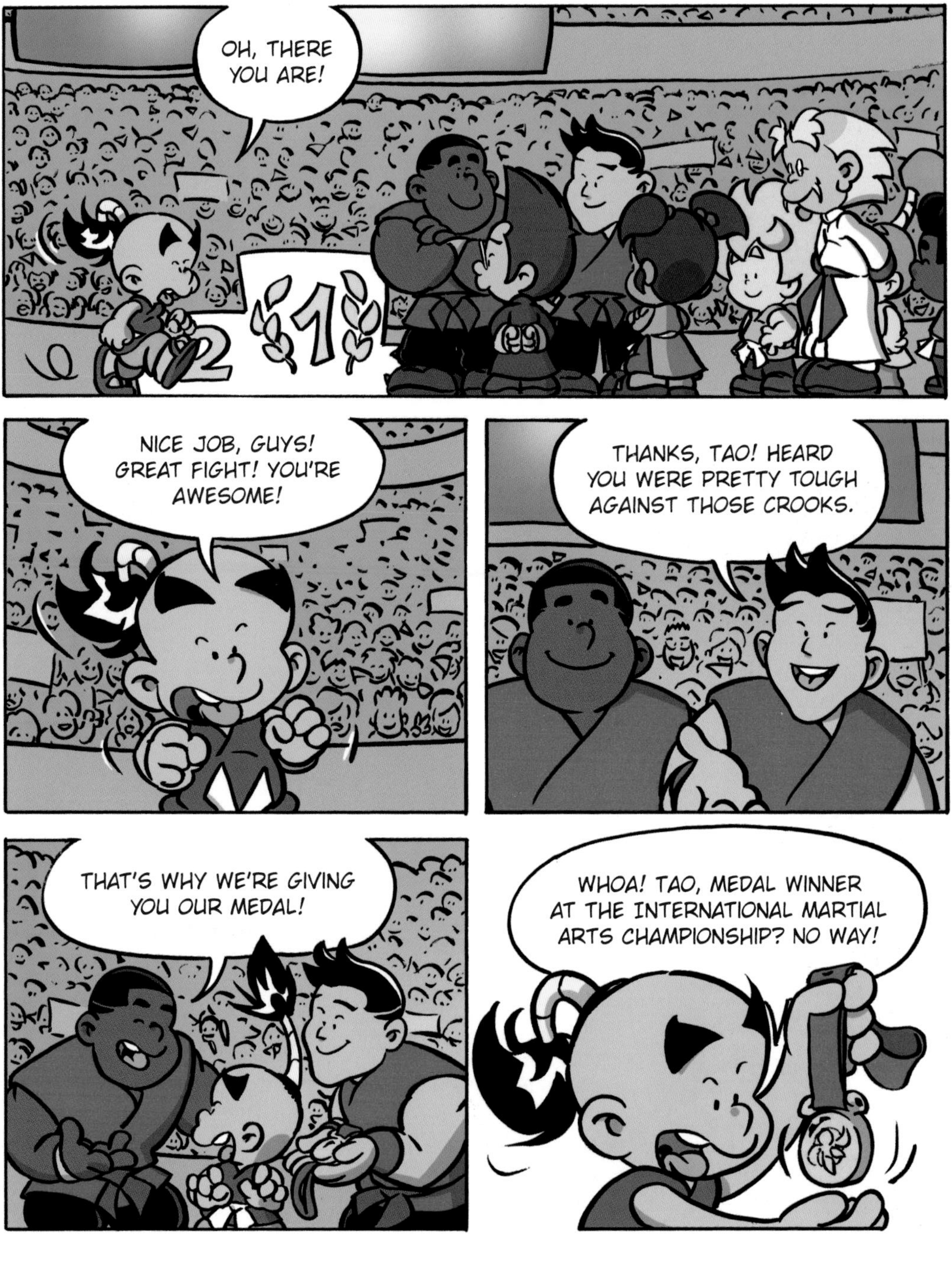
OH, THERE YOU ARE!
2
1
NICE JOB, GUYS! GREAT FIGHT! YOU'RE AWESOME!
THANKS, TAO! HEARD YOU WERE PRETTY TOUGH AGAINST THOSE CROOKS.
THAT'S WHY WE'RE GIVING YOU OUR MEDAL!
WHOA! TAO, MEDAL WINNER AT THE INTERNATIONAL MARTIAL ARTS CHAMPIONSHIP? NO WAY!

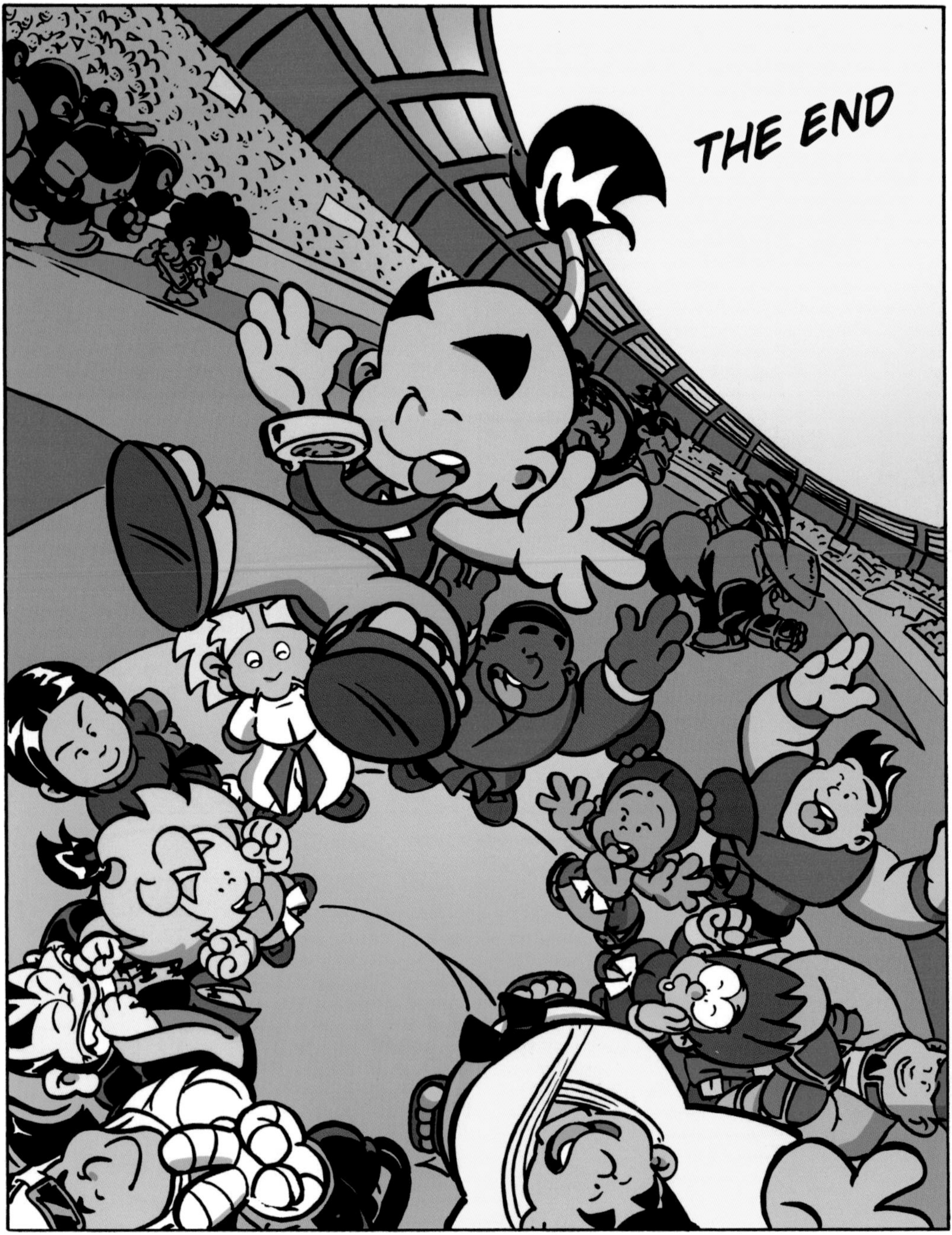
THE END

NIKO & LOLO

The Creators of Tao Present Their Desks!

WHAT A MESS!

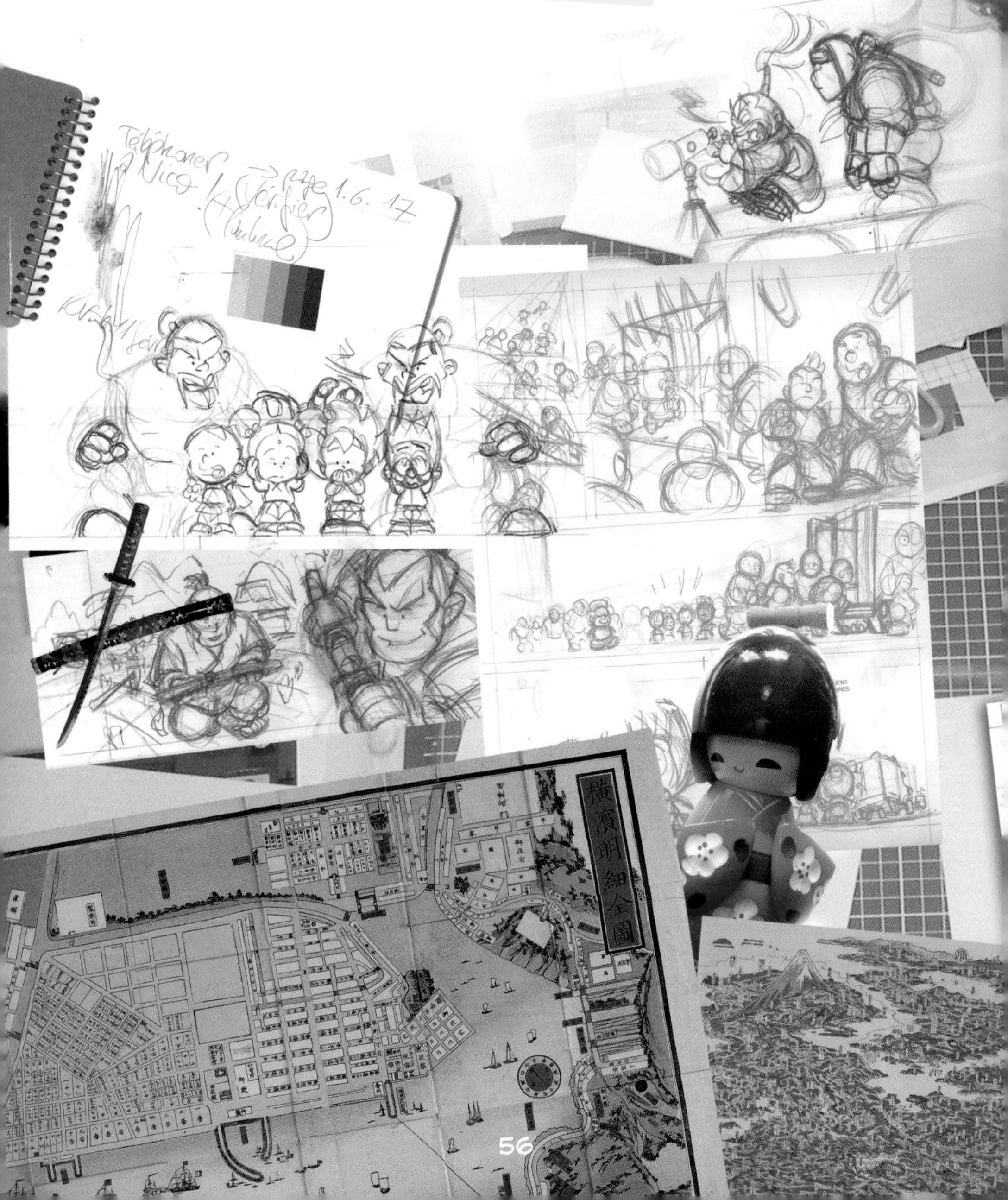

Téléphoner à Nico!
1.6.17
Vérifier
横濱明細全圖

ABOUT THE AUTHOR

Laurent Richard worked in the world of advertising before becoming a professor of graphic arts. He now divides his time between teaching and illustration for children's publishing and media.

ABOUT THE ILLUSTRATOR

Nicolas Ryser attended the School of Graphic Arts Estienne in Paris. He won several competitions including the Angoulême and works for the magazine *Casus Belli*. He was recently awarded a *Graine de pro* ("Seed of a professional") prize.

TAO
The Little Samurai